EGMONT

We bring stories to life

First published in Great Britain 2010 by Dean,
an imprint of Egmont UK Limited
239 Kensington High Street, London W8 6SA

Thomas the Tank Engine & Friends™

CREATED BY BRITT ALLCROFT

Based on The Railway Series by The Reverend W Awdry
© 2010 Gullane (Thomas) LLC. A HIT Entertainment company.

Thomas the Tank Engine & Friends and Thomas & Friends are trademarks of Gullane (Thomas) Limited.
Thomas the Tank Engine & Friends and Design is Reg. U.S. Pat. & Tm. Off.

HiT entertainment

ISBN 978 0 6035 6546 5
1 3 5 7 9 10 8 6 4 2
Printed and bound in China

Contents

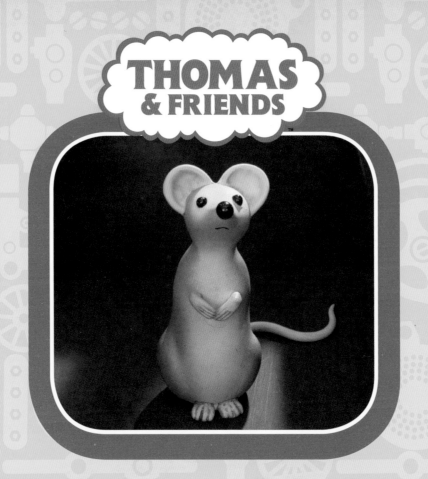

THOMAS & FRIENDS

Thomas, Percy and the Squeak

The engines on the Island of Sodor love the summer. Sometimes, The Fat Controller holds concerts.

One morning the engines were very excited. Alicia Botti, the famous singer, was coming to Sodor to sing at The Fat Controller's concert.

"I am bound to be chosen to collect her," boasted James. "I'm the brightest and the shiniest engine!"

"Nonsense! I'm the most important!" huffed Gordon.

Thomas wanted to feel important, too. "The Fat Controller might choose me," he said, hopefully.

Percy came along next to Gordon. His face was very grimy.

"Well, one thing's for sure," snorted Gordon. "He won't choose dirty Percy."

"I'm dirty because I work hard," said Percy, proudly. And he wheeshed away.

The next day, The Fat Controller came to decide which engine would collect the singer from the Docks.

He didn't choose Gordon.

And he didn't choose James.

He chose Thomas! "Make sure Annie and Clarabel are squeaky clean," he said.

"Yes, Sir!" said Thomas, excitedly. He felt very important indeed.

Thomas hurried off to the Wash to be cleaned. He wheeshed up next to Percy. "Move aside," said Thomas. "I'm the important engine today."

"But I need a washdown!" wailed Percy. "My passengers will laugh at me."

"You'll have to wait," huffed Thomas. "Today, I have to be squeaky clean."

"Then I'll have to go without being cleaned," said Percy, unhappily. "I'm a guaranteed connection!" He chuffed away, still very dirty.

Soon Thomas was squeaky clean and very shiny. He felt more important than ever.

But as the workers coupled Annie and Clarabel together, they heard a strange noise. A funny sort of squeak.

"What's that?" asked Thomas, anxiously.

His Driver quickly oiled Annie and Clarabel's undercarriage.

"That should take care of the squeak," said the Driver.

On the way to the Docks, Thomas heard the strange squeak again. He was worried now.

When he arrived, a big liner had brought lots of passengers to the Island of Sodor. Alicia Botti, the famous singer, was waiting with The Fat Controller.

Thomas squeaked into the quayside.

The Fat Controller held Clarabel's door open for his special guest. He was pleased to see Thomas looking so clean and shiny. But as Alicia Botti was boarding the train, she saw a mouse inside the carriage!

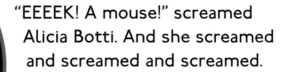

"SQUEAK!" said the mouse.

"EEEEK! A mouse!" screamed Alicia Botti. And she screamed and screamed and screamed.

She screamed so loudly and for so long that windows broke all over town. Alicia Botti was very cross indeed.

"I can't possibly travel in coaches full of mice," she said.

The Fat Controller was very embarrassed. Thomas didn't feel important anymore.

Just then, Percy returned from his guaranteed connection. He looked grimier than ever.

"Just look at that little green engine," Alicia Botti exclaimed. "So sweet . . . and dirty! Like a proper steam engine!"

The Fat Controller called Percy over at once. Alicia Botti boarded the train and Percy steamed away. He felt very proud.

Later that day, Thomas was waiting at the washdown when Percy chuffed up beside him.

"I'm sorry I was so cheeky," peeped Thomas. "You go first."

"Thanks, Thomas. It's good to be friends again," said Percy. "But where is your mouse?"

"You'll see!" grinned Thomas.

The Fat Controller had made the mouse her very own home in the corner of Tidmouth sheds. And Thomas named her Alicia.

THOMAS & FRIENDS

Gordon and Spencer

The Fat Controller's engines like doing special jobs for him. It makes them feel Really Useful and important!

One day, Gordon heard some very exciting news. He chuffed up alongside Thomas, who was waiting for his turn at the washdown.

"Move aside!" Gordon huffed. "This is a special day and I need to look my best!"

"**W**hy is it a special day?" Thomas asked.

"The Duke and Duchess are visiting the Island and The Fat Controller is sure to ask me to show them around," boasted Gordon. "After all, I am the fastest engine on the Island!"

Gordon was washed and scrubbed and polished until he was as shiny as a mirror. Then he rushed off to meet the Duke and Duchess.

Gordon was speeding happily towards Knapford Station when the signals turned red and Gordon was moved to a siding.

"What's going on?" puffed Gordon, crossly.

Suddenly there was a loud whoosh and a sharp whistle. A big silver engine rocketed past!

"Steaming pistons!" cried Gordon. "Who was that?"

When Gordon arrived at Knapford Station, he saw the sleek silver engine having a wash down and talking to James.

"Who are you?" Gordon asked.

"This is Spencer," James chuffed. "He's the fastest engine in the world!"

"I'm the Duke and Duchess's private engine," boasted Spencer. "I take them everywhere."

Gordon was disappointed. He wouldn't be showing the Duke and Duchess around the Island after all.

The Fat Controller came to see the engines.

"There will be a reception this afternoon for the Duke and Duchess at Maron Station," he said.

"That's the other side of Gordon's Hill," James explained to Spencer.

"You'll need to take on plenty of extra water," said Gordon, helpfully.

"I have plenty of water, thank you," wheeshed Spencer. He raced out of the yard with the Duke and Duchess aboard. Gordon felt sad. It wasn't going to be a special day for him after all.

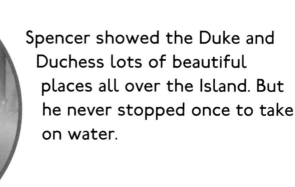

Spencer showed the Duke and Duchess lots of beautiful places all over the Island. But he never stopped once to take on water.

Gordon was dropping off some passengers at Wellsworth Station. He was feeling more miserable than ever.

"Make way!" boomed Spencer, racing past on his way to the reception.

"Big shiny show off!" Thomas snorted, as Spencer passed.

"Don't forget to take on some water!" whistled Gordon. But Spencer didn't listen.

When Spencer reached Gordon's Hill, he began to struggle. The hill grew steeper and steeper. And Spencer went slower and slower.

He puffed! He panted! He pulled with all his strength. But it was no use.

Spencer had run out of steam!

Spencer's Driver called The Fat Controller for help.
"I'll send one of my engines immediately," he promised.

The Stationmaster went to find Gordon. "The Fat Controller
has an important job for you," he said.
"An engine is stuck on a hill."

Gordon set off straight away.

Gordon was surprised to see Spencer stuck on the line! "What's wrong?" he asked.

"No water," Spencer snapped. "I must have a leaky tank."

"Perhaps," smiled Gordon. "But we'd better hurry. Everyone is waiting."

Gordon was soon coupled to Spencer, and they set off up the hill.

Gordon felt very proud as he pulled Spencer and his coaches into Maron Station. But Spencer just felt embarrassed!

"Well done, Gordon," said The Fat Controller. "You are a Very Useful Engine!"

They had arrived just in time for the start of the Duke and Duchess's grand reception!

"So, what do you think of Spencer now?" Thomas whispered to James.

"Too much puff and not enough steam!" laughed James.

"What about you, Gordon?" Thomas asked his friend.

But Gordon just smiled. It had turned out to be a special day, after all!

THOMAS & FRIENDS™

Diesel and the Troublesome Trucks

The engines that work on The Fat Controller's railway love feeling Really Useful.

The Troublesome Trucks are the opposite, they love being naughty and causing mischief. Sometimes they wear out the poor engines completely!

One day, The Fat Controller came to the shed to talk to the engines.

"Henry has broken down," he informed them.

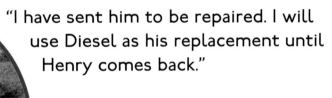

"I have sent him to be repaired. I will use Diesel as his replacement until Henry comes back."

"Yes, Sir," said the engines. But they weren't very happy.

The engines didn't like Diesel very much. He was very rude to them, and was always showing off.

"I hope Henry's mended soon," said Percy.

"He moves more trucks than three diesels put together," agreed Thomas, unhappily.

"Trucks are nobody's friends," puffed Gordon.

The next day, Diesel was working at the Docks.

"Wait until The Fat Controller sees how good I am," he boasted to the trucks. "He'll get rid of steam engines once and for all!"

This gave the trucks an idea.

As Diesel shunted the trucks together, they began to tease him.

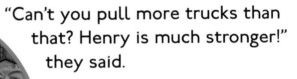

"Can't you pull more trucks than that? Henry is much stronger!" they said.

Diesel was very cross!

"I am stronger than Henry," snapped Diesel. "I could pull you all at the same time!"

The trucks giggled. "Pull us all! Pull us all! You'll be the strongest!" they chanted.

"That's me!" said Diesel. "The world's strongest engine!"

First, Diesel shunted five trucks together. Then ten.
Then fifteen.

Soon, he was preparing to shunt a very long line of twenty
Troublesome Trucks!

"What's Diesel doing?" asked Percy.

"He thinks he's the world's strongest engine," laughed Thomas.

Diesel tried to pull the long line of trucks. He pulled, and he pulled, and he pulled.

But the shunters had set the brakes on the trucks!

The trucks giggled. They tried to make Diesel pull them anyway.

"Pull! Pull! Pull!" they cheered.

Diesel pulled as hard as he could, but the trucks did not move.

Diesel was determined not to give up. He pulled, and he pulled, and he pulled with all his strength.

He pulled so hard that the couplings broke! SNAP! Diesel shot over the quayside and landed on Bulstrode the Barge!

"Ouch!" moaned Bulstrode.

The trucks laughed, and laughed, and laughed.

Just then, Henry arrived back from being repaired. The Fat Controller was on board. He looked down at Diesel, crossly.

"I thought you would be as good as Henry, but I was wrong!" said The Fat Controller. "I'm sending you home."

The Fat Controller turned to Henry. "Can you make up for lost time, Henry?" he asked.

"Oh yes, Sir!" replied Henry, happily.

Henry backed up to the long line of trucks, and the shunters released the brakes. Henry pulled the trucks easily! All the engines tooted and cheered.

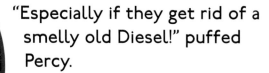

"Even Troublesome Trucks can be your friends!" laughed Thomas.

"Especially if they get rid of a smelly old Diesel!" puffed Percy.

THOMAS & FRIENDS

Emily's New Coaches

The engines were excited because a new engine was joining the Sodor Railway.

When Thomas came to Knapford Station he saw Emily, the new engine, waiting there. She was very smart with shiny brass fittings.

"Hello, I'm Thomas," wheeshed Thomas.

"Hello, I'm Emily," replied the new engine.

Thomas picked up his passengers and said goodbye to his new friend Emily.

Then The Fat Controller arrived to speak with her.
"Your new coaches are arriving at the Docks today, Emily. I want you to learn the passenger routes before they get here, so go out and collect any coaches you find and bring them back here."

"I will do that right away, Sir," said Emily.

The only coaches Emily and her Driver could find were Annie and Clarabel.

"Let's take these coaches back to the station," said Emily's Driver.

Annie and Clarabel were cross.

"It should be Thomas pulling us, not this strange new train," said Annie to Clarabel, but Emily did not hear her.

When Edward passed Emily he went to whistle "Hello" but then he saw she was pulling Annie and Clarabel.

He thought she had stolen Thomas' coaches, so when Emily peeped "Hello" to him, he just stared crossly at her.

And when Percy passed her later, he also scowled at her.

Emily wondered why everyone was being so rude to her.

Then Thomas came chuffing along the line towards her. Emily was pleased to see him because he had been so friendly that morning.

"Hello, Thomas," she peeped, cheerfully.

But to her surprise, Thomas glared at her and rushed past without saying a word.

Emily felt very sad. She thought no one liked her.

Later that day, The Fat Controller told Thomas to pick up the new coaches from the Docks.

"New coaches?" said Thomas. "But, I . . ."

"Really Useful Engines don't argue," said The Fat Controller, sternly.

Thomas set off grumpily. He didn't want new coaches, he wanted *his* coaches, Annie and Clarabel.

When Emily passed Tidmouth Sheds, Oliver said in surprise, "What are you doing with Thomas' coaches?"

"Oh!" said Emily. "Now I know why all the engines are so cross. The Fat Controller told me to pick up any coaches I could find, but I didn't realise these belong to Thomas. Everyone must think I've stolen them!"

Thomas collected the new coaches from the Docks.

They were shiny and smart, but Thomas didn't care.

"I don't want new coaches, I want *my* coaches!" he huffed to himself.

He was cross because he thought Emily had stolen Annie and Clarabel from him.

As Emily travelled to the station, a Signalman waved for her to stop.

"Oliver hasn't cleared his signal box," he said. "Please check what's wrong."

Oliver had broken down and was stuck on the crossing. Suddenly, Emily heard a whistle. Thomas was rushing towards Oliver.

He was braking hard, but he was going to crash into him!

Emily charged forward and with a burst of strength, pushed Oliver out of the way just in time.

Thomas came to a stop just behind her. He had had a lucky escape.

"Thank you," said Oliver. "You saved us from a really nasty accident."

"Yes, thank you," said Thomas, grumpily.

He was still upset because he thought Emily had taken his coaches.

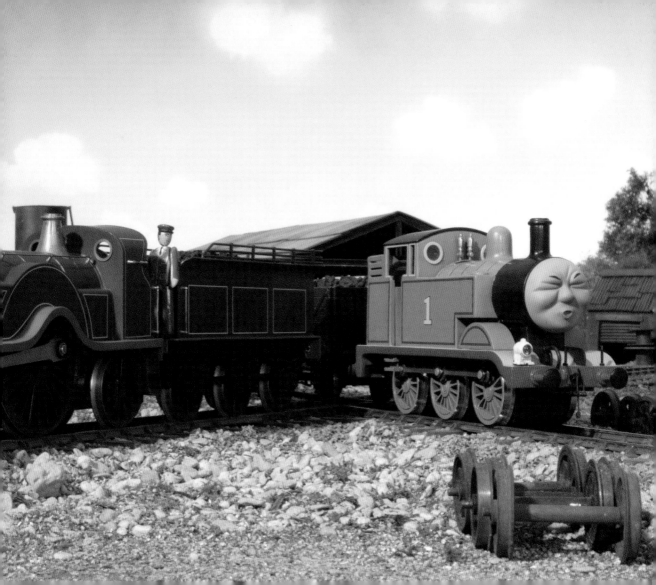

"I haven't stolen your coaches," Emily reassured Thomas. "I am taking them to the station like The Fat Controller asked me to."

"Oh!" peeped Thomas. Then he realised something.

"The new coaches I collected are for you, aren't they?" he asked.

"That's right!" laughed Emily. She was glad they were friends again.

"Hello," said Thomas, when Emily met him at the yard later on. "I have a surprise for you!"

"A surprise? For me?" said Emily, excitedly.

"Yes. We are all really happy that you've joined our Railway so we're having a party to welcome you!"

"Oh, thank you!" said Emily. She knew she was going to like working there with her new engine friends.